Three Fishes That Had Wishes

Jean Croak Atcherson

Illustrations by
Jan Carney

Cover Illustration by
Ann Hovey Amick

To order additional copies of this book, contact:
Xlibris
844-714-8691
www.Xlibris.com
Orders@Xlibris.com

ISBN: Softcover   978-1-6698-2087-1
         Hardcover   978-1-6698-2088-8
         EBook   978-1-6698-2086-4

Library of Congress Control Number: 2022907213

Print information available on the last page

Rev. date: 05/12/2022

For

George and Juliet, who taught me to see the beauty in the world and who always encouraged me to believe in myself and follow my dreams.

With all my love

In a beautiful neighborhood field filled with grasses and flowers, there lies a very special pond teeming with life and energy. The water in this pond is very clear and changes color throughout the day as the sun and the clouds pass by in the sky.

In the morning, as the sun rises, the water can be any shade of orange, yellow, or even pink. Throughout the day there are waves of blue, green, and even violet. At night stars can be seen through the midnight blue water and shed twinkling light upon the water.

If you look closely, beneath the surface, you will see an underwater world—a secret place full of life and activity. Everywhere you look, there is something happening. Plants sway on the currents, bubbles arise from the sand where residents are hiding, and turtles paddle near the surface, breathing the fresh air and looking at life outside the pond.

Many unique creatures live together in this pond's community, each with its own valuable role to play in this beautiful underwater world.

In this underwater world, there is a family of fishes with three new additions—Red Fish, Blue Fish, and Yellow Fish. Mother and Father Fish have been very busy with the three little ones, each unique and curious about the world around them.

The other residents of the pond were curious too. *Who were these new little fishes, and what would they do? It wouldn't be long until they would find out.*

Red Fish was the happy one and spent most of the day swimming around the pond. Red Fish used all the fins like wings, as if flying around the pond. By swishing the tail fin back and forth, Red Fish could create waves and make plants sway back and forth or sand to swoosh around the bottom of the pond. Red Fish thought, *I am so happy to be swimming around in my pond in all kinds of different ways. My wish is that everyone sees what a good swimmer I've become and that I can use this someday to help others.*

As they watched from afar, the other residents of the pond thought, *Red Fish seems to be wasting time just swimming around all day and should learn something useful.*

Mother and Father Fish loved Red Fish's uniqueness and said, "Let's just let nature take its course and see what happens."

Blue Fish was the friendly one and visited the other residents of the pond every day. Blue Fish knew everyone and discovered that all the pond residents were special, with their own places in the community. Listening to stories from the elders and caring for the young ones was how Blue Fish spent many days in the pond. Blue Fish loved these wonderful days and thought, *How lucky I am to be able to learn from and help those around me. My wish is to learn all I can about my community and those around me so that I can be helpful and do good for others someday.*

As they watched from afar, the other residents of the pond thought, *Blue Fish is wasting time all day just visiting and talking to others and should learn to do something useful.*

Mother and Father were proud of Blue Fish's uniqueness and said, "Let's just let nature take its course and see what happens."

Yellow Fish was the serious one and was always studying life in the pond. Yellow Fish studied the water, the structures and rock formations, the plant life, the sandy pond floor, and the ecosystem itself, documenting everything for further study to find out what they were made of as well as their role in the pond's community. Yellow Fish spent the days thinking, *How lucky I am to live in this beautiful world. My wish is to find out everything there is to learn and how by always learning more may help me to help those around me someday.*

Watching from afar, the other residents of the pond thought, *Yellow Fish is wasting time just looking around the pond all day and should learn to do something useful.*

Mother and Father Fish recognized Yellow Fish's uniqueness and said, "Let's just let nature take its course and see what happens."

And so the days and weeks passed by in this way for the three fishes that had wishes. As they grew bigger, they worked hard to develop their own special skills. Mother and Father Fish were very proud of their three fishes and their wishes, all of them unique in following their dreams.

All the residents of the pond watched everything the three fishes were doing as they became important members of their underwater community. They thought, *These three fishes had wishes, and they have worked hard to develop them and make them come true, each in their own way. Perhaps we were wrong in judging them too soon.*

Red Fish became the guardian of the pond and was able to alert the community when danger was near by calling everyone together with various signals, made by flapping different fins on the surface of the water. Red Fish also taught classes on pond safety, and the residents of the pond took basic training courses to learn how to help others in need and to help them escape from danger when needed.

Red Fish had always been a good swimmer, and taught the others swimming and exercising classes so they could stay in good shape and be fit. Red Fish thought, *My wish of being a good swimmer and using it to help others has come true. I worked hard to make my dream come true, and now the world is a better place.*

Blue Fish developed a special school for all the residents of the pond. Everyone found it easy to be around and talk to Blue Fish, who in turn made everyone feel special and important. They loved listening to stories about their history and learn the lessons about life in their pond. They learned how to care for each other and for their underwater world. Blue Fish had taught them to live together and contribute to the greater good of their shared community.

Blue Fish was always there to welcome new members and to make everyone realize they were important. Blue Fish thought, *My wish to learn more about my community in order to help others has come true because I worked hard to make it so. The world has become a better place now.*

Yellow Fish became a scientist and explorer, discovering new structures and uncovering artifacts and treasures all around the pond. Yellow Fish found new plants, rock formations and uncovered many new life forms. A good swish of the tail would move the sand around the pond floor, revealing fossils, gems, and sometimes residents hiding beneath the sand. There was a whole secret world to be uncovered and explored. Yellow Fish created a museum of the artifacts and history of the pond. The whole community learned about the pond's historical events, which helped them understand what made their underwater world what it is today.

Yellow Fish had always explored the underwater world, sharing the findings to help the others. Yellow Fish thought, *My wish of finding out everything I can about our world to help me be more useful to others has come true because I followed my dreams. I have made the world better by helping others understand the world around them and therefore themselves.*

These three fishes that had wishes became successful because they worked hard to follow their dreams and make their wishes come true.

Each of us has our own wishes and dreams inside. We are each as unique as these three fishes. Follow your own dreams, and always help others follow theirs, too. Be a good little fish in your life.

What are my dreams?

How can I accomplish my dreams?

Who can help me accomplish my dreams?

How can I help others accomplish their dreams?

How can I make the world a better place?

Printed in the United States
by Baker & Taylor Publisher Services